TRAPPED

Judy Spurr

iUniverse, Inc.
New York Lincoln Shanghai

Trapped

iUniverse books may be ordered through booksellers or by contacting:

iUniverse
2021 Pine Lake Road, Suite 100
Lincoln, NE 68512
www.iuniverse.com
1-800-Authors (1-800-288-4677)

Because of the dynamic nature of the Internet, any Web addresses or links contained in this book may have changed since publication and may no longer be valid.

This is a work of fiction. All of the characters, names, incidents, organizations, and dialogue in this novel are either the products of the author's imagination or are used fictitiously.

ISBN: 978-0-595-43915-7 (pbk)

ISBN: 978-0-595-88238-0 (ebk)

Printed in the United States of America

Acknowledgments

With thanks to my husband, Newt, who reread the manuscript countless times; my grandson, Ryan, and my young friend, Eric Radzinski, who both offered helpful insights and suggestions; and my writing cohorts, Eileen Mueller and Betty Ann St. Germain, who have been constant in their support and encouragement. Special thanks to my technical advisers, David Curley, Kenny Porter, Nancy Foster, and Patsy Whitlock.

CONTENTS

CHAPTER ONE

Fog drifted over Granite Cove harbor, wrapping the masts of the sailboats in its misty gray tentacles. I rowed the skiff out to our lobster boat. Voices of the fishermen in the boats around us dropped into the stillness.

While my dad and I waited for the fog to lift, I baited traps. Mac, our black Lab, jumped off the back of the boat for his morning swim. Head sticking out of the water, he paddled around with his mouth curved up as if he was smiling.

"Looks like the fog's lifting," Dad said and started the engine.

I lowered the ladder, and Mac climbed aboard.

"You've been a real help to me this summer, Jamie," Dad said. "I'll miss the extra pair of hands when you go back to school."

The foghorn on Thacher's Island wailed across the water. A cold feeling, like a lump of melting ice, spread through my stomach. Just thinking about school made me sick.

"I don't know why I have to go to school. I want to be a lobster-man like you."

"Lobsterin's a good life, Jamie, but not an easy one," he said. "Between government regulations and the cost of fuel, it's gettin' harder every day to pay the bills and have anything left over. You need to go to school." He turned away and restarted the engine.

My dad's blond hair curled around the edge of the Red Sox baseball hat he wore on the boat. He called it his lucky hat. He's more than six feet tall, with hands as big as oven mitts. Those hands would sure help me playing goalie in soccer.

All the years of pulling lobster traps had worn grooves into his palms. We had a hydraulic lift now to pull the pots. Up until a few years ago, he'd have to reach over the side of the boat, gaff the buoy, put the rope in the winch, and pull up each heavy trap hand-over-hand, sometimes for six or seven hours straight.

Lobsters stayed near shore at this time of year, so we didn't have to go out far to pull our traps. I took the wheel and steered next to the blue- and yellow-striped buoys that marked where we had dropped our pots. Dad shoved his red, chapped hands into thick rubber gloves and started the lift.

A lot of times, the pots would come up empty, but there were six lobsters in this one. They were crawling over each other trying to find a way out, but they were trapped. I knew how they felt because I felt trapped in school.

All morning, we moved from buoy to buoy, emptying traps. By the time we headed back to the harbor, bright sun had chased away the fog. In the afternoon sun, Granite Cove looked like a postcard. Fishing boats bobbed in front of the wharves lined with weathered gray shacks. Behind the docks, church steeples reached for the blue sky. Tourists snapped pictures or sat catching rays on the benches along the waterfront.

We unloaded our catch and headed for Olson's Fish Shack on Gull's Neck. Steam from lobsters boiling in a huge pot filled the small space. Ollie used to be a lobsterman. His long arms hung almost to his knees. He said his arms stretched every time he hauled a trap.

"Good catch today, Chris," Ollie wrote out a check and handed it to my father. "You lobstermen are keeping me in business. It's getting harder every day to get haddock. I know there aren't enough out there, but the latest regulations are squeezing us to death."

"I heard Len Ericson is thinking of selling his boat," Dad said.

"He's talking about it."

"That's a real shame," Dad said. "He's been fishing all his life, and his father and grandfather before him." Dad tucked the check into his shirt pocket. "See you Thursday."

"You're not going to have to sell your boat, are you?" I hurried to keep up as he strode across the pier.

"I don't plan to. Lobsterin' has always fed us and kept a roof over our heads, but there's not much left over after all the bills are paid."

I couldn't imagine my dad and me not working on the ocean, with waves splashing over the deck and the taste of salt spray on my tongue. When the sea was calm, the boat rocked back-and-forth like a cradle. In a storm, it rode the waves like a bucking bronco.

"Why does Mr. Ericson have to sell his boat?" I asked.

"It's complicated," he said. "Folks all over New England make their living fishing, and there just aren't enough fish in the area any more. The government sets limits on the amount of fish that can be caught legally. That means a lot of fishermen can't make enough money to keep their boats running and support their families."

"That's stupid," I said.

"That's what I thought at first, but there really is a shortage. If limits mean there will be enough fish and lobster left for your generation, then regulations make more sense. It sure hurts a lot of folks now, though."

We usually listened to country music in the truck, but neither of us turned on the radio. My dad was quiet, probably thinking about Mr. Ericson losing his boat. I was thinking about the summer-league soccer championship game that night. My team hadn't made it into the playoffs. We started the season with four straight wins, but then some of the players went on vacation with their families. It made me mad. They just didn't take summer soccer seriously. I hoped it would be different on the middle school team.

∗   ∗   ∗   ∗

"Please don't slam the door, Jamie," my mother said as the kitchen door banged behind me. She stood on a ladder with a paintbrush in her hand. Flecks of white paint dotted her hair and glasses.

"So, how did it go today?" She waved the brush in the air as she turned to talk to me. I ducked to miss the paint splatters.

"Okay," I said.

"Would you get me some tomatoes from the garden?" she asked. "I want to finish painting this wall before dinner."

"I've got a wicked headache," I said. "I'll get them later."

"It must be your allergies." She always blamed my headaches on allergies. "I keep hoping you'll outgrow them." Her voice followed me up the stairs. "You've certainly grown out of all your clothes. We'll have to go to the mall on Saturday. And you need a haircut!"

It was better not to argue with her—like when she said that we had to go to the mall and get clothes. If I told her that I didn't want to go to the mall because I thought the clothes I had were just fine, she'd say we'd have to go shopping tomorrow. If I said nothing, maybe she'd forget about it.

It wasn't easy being an only child. My friend Jake had six brothers and sisters. He thought I was lucky, but there's a lot of pressure when your parents only have one kid to worry about. They kind of overdo it.

I looked in the mirror in the upstairs hall to see if I needed a haircut. I saw a long, bony face with blond hair almost covering pale blue eyes. She was right about the haircut, but I didn't need to go clothes shopping. I hated shopping for anything, never mind clothes. I added having a haircut and going shopping to the list of reasons why I didn't want to go back to school.

I shouldn't have told her about the headache. She'd want to take me to the doctor. The doctor would pat me on the head and give me some pills, but I had the headache because school was starting.

I hated school. I started hating it in second grade when we took turns reading aloud. When I read, I made up most of the words, and the whole class laughed at me. Ray Quinn called me a dummy.

That's why I couldn't stand Ray Quinn. He was on my soccer team, so I had to see him all the time. We were both goalies, and this summer, I was the starting goalie. He wasn't too happy about that.

Mac jumped up on the bed and laid his head on my pillow. I scratched his back. His fur was stiff after his swim.

"School's starting next week, Mac. I won't be around much."

He pushed his face under my chin and whimpered, as if he understood.

CHAPTER TWO

When the alarm went off on the first day of school, I stared at the cracks on the bedroom ceiling. They looked like a tic-tac-toe game. I dragged myself out of bed, pulled on jeans and a shirt, and followed the smell of bacon to the kitchen. We only had bacon on special days. I guess Mom thought the first day of school was special. Not me.

"What were they thinking?" I complained, after eating a stack of pancakes and a gazillion pieces of bacon. "We never go back to school before Labor Day. It's stupid," I grumbled. "I'm not going today. I'll start next week. I need to help Dad."

"School starts today, Jamie." My mother held open the screen door and handed me lunch in a brown paper bag. At least she hadn't tried to put it in my *Star Wars* lunch box.

Dad and Mac were waiting for me in the truck. Mac climbed onto my lap. I buried my face in his fur. It smelled of wet leaves and dirt.

"You need to hustle in the morning, Jamie. I'm not usually around to give you a ride, and your mother has to get to work." Dad jammed the truck into gear.

"What are you going to do without me all day, Mac?"

"He's coming out on the boat with me," Dad said. "That dog has figured every way there is to get out of the yard. Unless we lock him in the house, he'll wander all over town. I've never seen a dog like him."

It was true. Mac was like Houdini. In first grade, he came to school and waited outside for me until recess. He was a great climber. He could hop right up the ladder to the slide and whiz down as good as any kid. He even ran the bases during kickball games, until the principal called my mother. She told her Mac was a talented dog, but he needed to stay at home during school hours.

That's when we built the fence around the yard. He learned how to climb out of that on the first day. Then we put a run in the fenced area, but he managed to slip out of every collar and climb the fence anyway.

"You just like people, don't you, Mac?" He turned and gave me a sloppy Mac kiss.

Breakfast began flipping around in my stomach as we pulled up in front of the middle school. When I opened the door to get out, Mac jumped over me and galloped toward a group of girls standing in front of the main door. I ran after him. He'd stop, and as soon as I caught up to him, he'd run off again.

The girls giggled. I felt my face getting red. One of the girls was Chrissie Young, who wasn't exactly a girlfriend—more like a friend who is a girl. I felt like a jerk.

By the time I got Mac into the truck, I had missed the first bell. When I finally found my homeroom, there were three seats left, all of them in the front row. Ray Quinn was in one of them. I didn't like sitting in the front row, and I sure wasn't happy Ray was in my homeroom. I didn't look at him, and he didn't look at me.

I didn't have to. I knew what he looked like. He always needed a haircut. He wore jeans and a Miami Dolphins T-shirt to school every day, except in the winter, when he changed the T-shirt for a Dolphins sweatshirt. He was probably the only kid in school who wasn't a New England Patriots fan. His feet were stuck out in front of him, ready to trip the first unfortunate person who crossed his path.

Just as the second bell blasted in my ear, a little kid who looked like he should be in elementary school came skidding into the room. His hair was the color of my mother's tomatoes. Freckles as big as dimes stuck out all over his face. He stepped over Ray's feet and sat between us.

"You must be Oscar," Mr. Bracken said to the new kid as he handed us our schedules.

"That's me," the kid said.

"So, Oscar," Ray whispered to the new kid. "How are things on Sesame Street?"

"Don't know," Oscar whispered back, grinning at Ray.

Here's the new target, I thought. He sure had a lot of confidence for a new kid. Ray would probably knock that out of him pretty quick.

Learning Center and Reading Tutorial jumped off the page of my class schedule. I'd been going to the learning center for extra help since I was in second grade. I had hoped middle school would be different, like they wouldn't have a learning center and everyone would forget I'd ever gone there.

"The reading tutor's name is Mrs. Hogan. Her office is near the gym," Mr. Bracken said quietly as I headed out the door. Of course, big-ears Ray heard.

"Loser," he whispered.

The headache gremlins began pounding a tune in my head. I was sure I was going to throw up.

I had a hard time finding the reading tutor's room. They'd stuck her next to the gym office at the other end of the school. She didn't look much like a teacher. She looked like somebody's grandmother, although my grandmother wouldn't be caught dead with that long skirt and "Save the Whales" T-shirt.

"I've looked at your records, Jamie," she said. "Math and science seem to be your strengths. I think we can work together to help you read more easily and improve your grades in your other classes."

Blah, blah, blah. I'd heard the same speech every year with every reading teacher I'd ever had. None of them could break through the cement in my head when it came to making sense of all those squiggles on the page. It wasn't until third grade that I figured out there was a space between the words. I thought they all just ran together. The teachers call it dyslexia. It sounds like some kind of disease, but it isn't. It sure makes school harder, though.

The teacher picked up some cards with letters on them. She held up a card with an *a* on it and told me the sound.

"I *know* the alphabet!" I wasn't going to sit there while she flashed cards in my face like I was in first grade.

"This isn't going to work," I said under my breath.

"Trust me," she said and held up a card, gave me the sound, and asked me to repeat it. The clock on her desk ticked loudly into the silence. She put down the cards, folded her hands on the desk, and leaned toward me. Her eyes were almost black. When she looked into my eyes, it was if she could see what I was thinking.

"Jamie, your reading difficulties mean that you missed something in earlier grades. I need to find out what that is and work from there."

I crossed my arms over my chest, narrowed my eyes, and put a leave-me-alone look on my face.

"I'm going to give you a passage to read. Then I can decide where we should begin."

She handed me a sixth-grade social studies book. The first page looked easy—all small words, lots of pictures. I turned to the next page, and I couldn't read the first word. She told me it was hemisphere and that we would be studying the Western Hemisphere this year in social studies.

I stumbled over about half of the words on the page.

"The longer words give you trouble, Jamie," she said. "I can help you learn to break those words into parts called syllables."

"I'll also speak to your English teachers to find out what books you're reading and order them on tape. It will save a lot of time when you only have a week or two to read a book for an assignment."

That was the first good idea I'd heard all day.

The next thirty minutes dragged. I was not interested in learning about the six kinds of syllables, not to mention suffixes and prefixes. I didn't need to know about them. I just needed to figure out how to read them. It didn't look like this lady was going to be much help to me. I jumped up when the bell rang.

"I'll see you tomorrow, Jamie," she said as I fled the room.

Not if I can help it, I thought.

The rest of the day wasn't so bad. Math and science went okay. Nobody asked me to read in any of my classes. The social studies teacher, Mr. Sparks, seemed more like an actor than a teacher. When he talked about the Pilgrims landing at Plymouth, he paced back-and-forth at the front of the room and waved his arms as if he had been on board the Mayflower himself.

Since I brought my lunch, I decided to eat outside. The lunch monitor came out and told me there's a rule in middle school that you have to eat in the cafeteria. Dumb rule if you ask me.

When I went into the cafeteria, I saw Sam Roberto and Jake Fletcher at a table in the far corner. Jake had been on my soccer team in the spring, and I liked him. He went to his grandmother's farm in New Hampshire for the summer. I hadn't seen him since school got out.

"Hey, how's it going, Jamison?" Jake asked when I went over to their table.

"Okay. Had a good summer. I worked with my dad on the boat. How about you guys?"

"Pretty good," Jake said. "It was kind of boring at my grandparents. Not much to do. Their little town doesn't even have summer soccer."

"Did you play, Jamie?" Sam asked.

"Yeah, I did. We had a good season, but we didn't get into the playoffs. We needed good players like Jake, who took off for the summer."

"Maybe my folks will stay home next year," Jake said.

"Were you in goal?" he asked.

"Yeah."

"Bet old Ray Quinn was mad."

"He played some," I said.

"Can I sit here?" I looked up, and the new kid was putting his tray down on the table.

"Sure. I mean, I guess so," I said.

Sam and Jake stared at Oscar. I wasn't the only one who thought the new kid looked weird with that red hair sticking up all over his head.

Oscar was still eating when the three of us went outside to kick a soccer ball around.

"Where's that kid from, Jamie?" Jake asked, dribbling the ball across the grass.

"His hair's so red you almost need sunglasses to look at him. Is he a friend of yours?" Sam asked.

"No. He isn't," I said quickly, so they wouldn't connect me with this kid. I had enough problems of my own. "He's in my home-room. I never saw him before this morning."

"So, are you going to try out for the middle-school soccer team?" I asked Jake.

"Sure. I'm rusty, though. Who played center striker this summer?"

"Chuck Santo," I said. "He's good."

"I'll never get to play," Jake moaned.

"He's a freshman at the high school," I said. "So he won't be on the middle-school team."

"Great!" Jake smiled.

The bell rang, and we headed back to afternoon classes.

At the end of the day, I couldn't wait to get out of the place. I hurried to my locker, but the piece of paper that I'd written the combination on wasn't in my pocket. The building was almost empty by the time I found the paper stuck into my social studies book.

My dad's truck was parked at the end of the school driveway. Mac jumped out the open window and ran around me in circles.

He climbed onto my lap when I got in the car.

"Mac, you're a goof," I said.

"How'd it go?" Dad asked.

"Okay," I said. "But, ah … there's this reading teacher they sent me to, and I know she's not going to help, so can you call and get me out of that class?"

"I don't want to do that, Jamie. I know school is really hard for you," he said. "I remember what it was like to be your age and struggling to read, but they didn't understand dyslexia back then. Now there are teachers trained to help people learn to read. You're luckier than I was, but you need to work as hard in school as you do with me when we're on the boat."

Dad usually understood how I felt about school, but he sure wasn't acting like it right then. I didn't want to talk about school. I just wanted to go home, grab my bike, and let the wind blow the chalk dust out of my brain.

Mac and I rode into the woods. It had rained earlier, but patches of sunlight filtered through the last few clouds. The woods felt like another world. Only bird chatter and wind humming through the trees broke the silence.

CHAPTER THREE

The next morning, Mac jumped up on the bed and woke me with a slobbery Mac-kiss on my nose. I had been dreaming I was playing a soccer game. I'd just saved a goal and was kicking the ball downfield, but it kept coming back and hitting me on the head.

Middle school started one whole hour earlier than elementary, which is why I had a hard time getting out of bed. I put my arm around Mac and dozed off again.

"Are you ready for breakfast?" Mom called up the stairs.

Before I could answer, she came into my room and began yanking open bureau drawers.

"Honestly, Jamie. You aren't even out of bed." Shirts, underwear, and jeans all landed on my bed in a heap.

"It's seven o'clock. Get moving."

I wanted to tell her I hated school. I think I was probably the only kid in sixth grade that went to a special reading teacher. As usual, she read my mind. She closed the bureau drawer and sat down at the foot of the bed.

"I know what you're feeling. Dad told me you didn't want to go to the reading teacher," she said. "You do have a harder time reading than most of the other kids, but that doesn't mean they're smarter than you. It's up to you to prove that. This new teacher might be just the person who can help you." She patted my leg under the covers.

"Come on. Get dressed. I'll give you a ride."

When I went downstairs, she stood at the kitchen door, jiggling her keys. No time for bacon today. I grabbed a banana out of the bowl on the kitchen table and ate it in the car.

Halfway to school, I saw the new kid walking on the side of the road. I couldn't miss that neon-red hair.

"That must be the boy who moved into Burke's farm," my mother said and slammed on the brakes.

"What are you doing?"

"I'm going to offer him a ride to school."

"You don't even know him." I shrank down in the seat.

"No, but I know he's new in town, and he'll probably be late for school if we don't give him a ride."

I don't know why she does these things. She talks to strangers in checkout lines at the supermarket too.

Oscar climbed into the backseat.

"Thanks for picking me up. I overslept, which I do a lot."

"Jamie does too," she said, turning around with one hand on the steering wheel. Someday, she's going to drive off the road trying to talk to someone in the backseat.

"I met your mother at the market yesterday," she told him. "We live at the end of this road, just before the entrance to South Woods.

Your house has been empty for quite a while. It's nice to have neighbors again."

"Uh, Mom." I interrupted her before she invited him over for milk and cookies after school. "Don't forget to put Mac in the house."

"I won't."

She turned into the school driveway, barely missing a parked school bus. I closed my eyes.

"Thanks for the ride, Mrs. Parker." Oscar slammed the car door.

"Who's Mac?" he asked.

"Our dog. He's a black Lab. If we leave him out, he climbs right over the fence. He either comes to school or goes downtown to the store where my mother works."

"Sounds like a smart dog," he said.

"He is, but one of the clueless tourists zooming through town could hit him, so we try to keep him in the house when we're not around."

The bell rang. Kids stampeded into the building. Locker doors banged open and shut. Books dropped. Girls giggled. It was noisy— a lot noisier than elementary school.

"Good morning, O-s-car-r." Ray stood next to his locker. "Good morning, Big Bird." Ray looked right at me. Was he calling me Big Bird?

"Hey, Oscar. Do you think they can teach Big Bird to read on Sesame Street?"

I clenched my fist and headed toward Ray. He backed away, grinning.

"Jamie!" Mr. Bracken came out of his room in time to see me raise my fist. "What's this all about?"

I dropped my arm and put my hands in my pockets.

"Ray's being a jerk," Oscar said.

"Boys, it's just the second day of school. You're going to have to find a way to get along."

He pointed his finger at Ray. "No more smart remarks from you, wise guy."

Ray's smirk shrunk.

Mr. Bracken turned to me. Even through his thick glasses, I could feel the glare. "And Jamie, don't even think of fighting in school."

I'd never thought of fighting in or out of school before, but I couldn't keep taking Ray's bullying.

"Get to class, the three of you," he barked.

At the end of the day, when I tried to open my locker, the handle was covered with gum.

"What's that on your hands?" Oscar's locker was next to mine.

"Gum."

"Gum on your fingers? You're supposed to chew it—in your mouth."

"No kidding. This isn't my gum. Someone put it on the lock."

"Gross!"

I washed my hands in the boys' bathroom and rubbed at the gum with a paper towel, but I couldn't get it all off.

Oscar waited for me outside.

"What is with that Quinn kid?" he asked.

"He's a bully."

"Yeah, I know he is, but what else does he do, besides mouth-off and put gum on locks and find people to push around?"

"Stuff," I said.

This kid was quick. He figured out right away that it was probably Ray Quinn who put the gum on my locker.

A bunch of seagulls screamed overhead. I ducked. Flying seagulls have been known to drop a load on whatever happens to be underneath.

"Like what kind of stuff?"

"Last year, he took my bike for a ride around the parking lot and rammed it into the bike rack. The bumper had a huge dent, paint was scratched up, and the air leaked out of the front tire. I had to push it all the way home. I'd worked all summer to buy that bike."

"But why? Why does he pick on you?"

I didn't want to go into the whole history of Jamie Parker and Ray Quinn. This kid was probably the only one in my class who didn't know I couldn't read too well.

"He always picks on kids smaller than him," I said.

"You're not smaller than him," Oscar said. "Why do you think he calls you Big Bird?"

He was right. I had grown a few inches over the summer.

"So Ray is picking on me because I'm small and my name's Oscar. Right?"

"Right."

"So why is Quinn still bugging you?"

"Well, he wasn't real happy that I was the starting goalie on the summer soccer team. He was the backup."

"Oh, great! He plays soccer. Now he can hassle me on the field too."

I looked at Oscar and wondered how he'd ever play on a middle-school team. He was much shorter than any of the other players.

"What position do you play?" I asked.

"You know for sure I'm not a center striker," he said. "I'll play wherever the coach puts me."

"I hope I get a chance to play in goal," I said.

"Do you know who your competition is?" he asked.

"There's Ray and another kid, Hank Miller, who's in eighth grade. He played summer soccer, too, but he was on another team."

"Fighting won't stop Ray, you know," Oscar said. "He'd love a fight." He ran his fingers through his hair, making it stick up worse than ever.

"If you can come up with a better way, let me know," I said.

"I will," he said, turning up the driveway. "See ya."

He wasn't so bad, even if he had blazing red hair that stuck up all over his head as if he'd put his finger in an electrical socket.

CHAPTER FOUR

Soccer practice started the second week of school. Oscar and I were the first ones at the field. Coach was setting up cones for practice drills when we got there.

I stood in goal, and Oscar took some shots. He looked even smaller on the soccer field, but if he could move, his size might be a bonus.

He slammed the ball into the back left corner of the net.

"Not bad," I said.

"Not bad? That was a great shot," Oscar said, grinning.

"Hey, stick legs, watch the ball," Ray called from the sidelines.

"Either put on a pair of shorts and come to practice or get out of here, Ray," Coach Curran yelled across the field.

Maybe Ray wasn't coming out for soccer. I figured Hank Miller would probably have the job of starting goalie, but I'd have a lot more playing time if Ray wasn't on the team. Hank was a good goalie. He was a big kid—not real tall, but he was solid.

"Okay, you guys. Let's begin with an attack-and-defense drill; then we'll play flag soccer," Coach called out.

Ray came back on the field in his shorts. So much for more playing time!

"You're late, Quinn," Coach said. "Get here at 2:30 sharp, or don't bother to come."

After about forty minutes of practice drills, Coach called for a scrimmage.

There's no goalie in a scrimmage, so neither Ray nor I had a chance to show Coach what we could do.

He blew the whistle to end practice and called Hank, Ray, Jake, Rob Cody, Lou Paulson, and me over.

"Plan to stay later tomorrow afternoon," he said. "I want to look at each of you. Hank's the starting goalie, and Rob will start as center striker. I know Ray and Jamie want a chance in goal, and Jake and Lou Paulson hope to have of some time at center striker."

"At least we have a chance." I high-fived Jake as we headed for the locker room.

"Probably not much playing time, though," Jake said.

When I opened my locker after I got out of the shower, it was empty. I pulled the towel around me and checked the number again. Right number, but I hadn't clicked the lock.

"You planning on wearing that towel home?" Oscar poked his head around the corner.

I pointed to the empty locker. "I didn't lock it, and someone took my clothes."

"What are you guys still doing in here?" Coach didn't look too happy when he came out of the gym office and found Oscar and me in the locker room.

I explained.

"Oscar, check the trash. The clowns that play this trick usually just dump the clothes in the nearest wastebasket."

We checked all the wastebaskets in the gym. No clothes.

"I'll check the hall," Oscar said.

"Found them." He handed me my clothes.

"Next time, use the lock," Coach said.

"I bet Ray took your stuff when he came in to dress," Oscar said as we took the shortcut across the field behind the bleachers.

"Yeah, but we can't prove it. You're right that he's just looking for a fight, but if I don't stand up to him sooner or later, it's just going to get worse."

"But Ray, honey. Why can't you come to the dance Friday night?"

Ray? Honey? Oscar and I looked up at the bleachers. There was old Ray, sitting with Chrissie Young.

Oscar doubled over, laughing. I didn't feel much like laughing. Ray Quinn with Chrissie Young? Oscar snorted real loud when he laughed. Ray heard him.

"Hey, what's going on?" Ray glared down at us.

"Nothing, honey," Oscar said, still laughing. He and I took off across the field.

"Boy, did we just get lucky!" Oscar said. "We can call him 'honey' whenever he bugs us. I love it!"

I didn't say anything. I couldn't figure out how a nice girl like Chrissie would hang around with Ray, *and* she called him "honey."

Oscar was still chuckling when my father came along. "You two want a ride?" he asked.

We climbed in the front seat, and Mac sat in back with the traps.

"Is that what you catch lobsters in?" Oscar asked. "I've only seen lobsters in pictures."

"Where did you live before you came to Granite Cove?" Dad asked him.

"Colorado," he said. "My mom grew up here in New England, and she wanted to live near family again."

"Why don't you come out on the boat with us Saturday?" Dad asked. "We can always use the help."

"I'd love to," Oscar said. "What time?"

"About 6:00 a.m.," Dad said.

"I'll be ready."

*   *   *   *

Saturday morning, rivers of rain ran down the driveway and played drumbeats on the hood of the truck as we jolted in and out of ruts in the dirt road. Mac bounced up-and-down on the seat next to me.

"Is this storm going to last?" I asked. We usually didn't go out in bad weather.

"Forecast says the rain will stop midmorning. I'm not going out far," he answered. "I need to empty a few pots around the island. If it's too rough, we'll come back in. When we're finished, you and Oscar can give the boat a good cleaning."

Oscar stood at the end of his driveway, waiting for us. Water from his slicker dripped all over the seat of the truck.

"Nice boat," Oscar said when we rowed out to our mooring.

"I've only had this one a few years," Dad told him. "I held on to a wooden boat longer than most people did, but fiberglass needs a lot less work."

Rain didn't seem to bother Oscar. Neither did a choppy sea. By the time we left the dock, the rain had stopped, but the surf was still heavy. I figured he would get sick for sure, but even baiting the traps didn't bother him, and that stuff smelled bad.

"You two check these," Dad said, then dropped the flailing lobsters into the catch box. Their claws clicked across the plastic bottom.

"We have to throw them back unless they measure at least 3 ¼ inches from their eyes to the beginning of their tails," I explained to Oscar." We can't keep females with eggs on the underside of their tails, either."

"Hey, look at this guy kick." One of the bigger lobsters waved his claws as Oscar held it in the air.

"Get those rubber bands on his claws, or he'll take a piece of you," Dad told him.

The first one I picked up clawed at the air and flapped its tail against my arm.

"I've been nipped a few times when I didn't get these rubber bands onto their claws quick enough," I told Oscar. "Last summer one got me. My finger swelled up to the size of a hot dog. Man was I sick! I took some pills, and the swelling went down, but I learned the hard way to be quicker than they are."

By the end of the morning, Oscar banded lobsters as if he'd been doing it all his life.

"How do they taste?" he asked.

"Most people around here like 'em," Dad said.

When we got back to the dock, Dad took the catch to Olson's. Oscar and I washed down the boat.

"Lot of boats in here," Oscar said.

"Not as many as there used to be," I told him. "Some of the fishermen have had to sell their boats."

"Why?"he asked. "Don't people eat as much fish anymore?"

"No. That's not it," I said. "People eat more fish and lobsters. There aren't as many as there used to be, so the government made rules about how much can be caught, and it's harder for the fisher men to make money."

"Too bad," Oscar said.

Lobstermen sat along the dock weaving nets, fixing broken lobster traps, and swapping stories. I could hear my father's laugh boom across the cove. I figured it was a good sign if he was laughing. He'd been pretty quiet lately. Two more Granite Cove fishermen had sold their boats and started a job-training program. Mr. Ericson was going to be a welder.

Sun had burned the clouds away. The smell of rotting fish and dried seaweed hung in the air. We stored the last of the gear in our shack and sat on the edge of the dock. I looked across at the headlands, where a couple of seagulls were screeching at each other fighting over a clamshell.

"That was really fun today," Oscar said. "It's probably not so much fun in bad weather."

"No, then the ocean can be really scary," I said.

"You ever get caught in a storm?" he asked.

"My dad's been in some bad ones," I said. "The worst one for me was last July."

"What happened?" he asked.

"It was a great day—clear sky, not a ripple on the ocean. All of a sudden, a wall of fog moved in. I could hear the foghorn moaning, but it didn't sound like it was coming from the right direction. I knew we weren't far from land, but the breakwater was close too. If we hit it, the boat could break up, but my dad kept his cool and maneuvered into the cove just about blindfolded."

"My dad died," Oscar said. He hung his hands between his legs and stared down into the water.

I looked at the fish swimming under the wharf and listened to the water slapping against the pilings. I tried to think of something to say.

His words hung in the air between us.

"When?" I asked finally.

"Last winter. We were on our way home from skiing. It was snowing, and we drove into a whiteout. A truck skidded into the side of the car. We weren't as lucky as you and your dad."

He stopped and looked out over the cove as if he was looking at a picture in his head—a picture he'd probably looked at a million times in the past year.

Why did I just tell him that story? I asked myself.

"My mom broke both her legs," he continued. "My little sister Beth had a concussion. The rest of us didn't even get a bloody nose. It doesn't seem right, does it?"

He looked at me as if I might have an answer to the question he'd probably been asking himself since the accident.

I didn't.

CHAPTER FIVE

I felt different about Oscar after the day on the boat—not just because his father died, but because he was the first close friend I'd ever had. Besides, he was funny. He'd tell a story, and halfway through, he'd begin to laugh. When he laughed, he snorted, and you had to laugh with him.

The other kids had stopped treating him like the new kid, but Ray kept up with the Big Bird/*Sesame Street* routine, although no one listened to him, except me.

Sitting on the bench with Ray in soccer bothered me the most. He badmouthed everyone.

"Hank just doesn't have the moves to be a goalie," he'd say. "He's slow. Why did Coach pick him? Even Big Bird is better than him, and that's not saying much."

Hank wasn't fast, but he did manage to make a lot of saves, and that's what counts.

League rules say that everyone on the team had to play at least ten minutes a game. I played defense, but not in goal. Oscar got more playing time than I did. His size confused the opposite teams' players. They couldn't believe it when he'd pop the ball from between their legs and run upfield, handing it off to a winger or striker.

A couple of games were rained out. They rescheduled one for a Saturday in mid-October. The sun was out, the sky was blue, and the stands were full. My dad sat in the front row of the bleachers. I told him I probably wouldn't play, but he said he was there to support the team.

"You'll have your chance," he said.

Sitting on the bench was even harder when I knew my father was there.

With three minutes to go in the second half, Coach put Oscar in at right wing. We were ahead 3–1. Oscar was all over the place, scooping the ball from under the players' legs, setting up Rob for shots on goal. I sat on the bench, sweating in the sun.

"I can't believe Coach puts that little squirt in before me," Ray said. "I can move the ball. He's just not giving me a chance."

"Thought you wanted to play goalie," I said.

I almost added "honey" at the end, but Coach wouldn't think much of a fight on the bench during a game.

"Yeah, but I hate being a bench jockey," he replied. "And it looks like old Hank the turtle has goal all sewed-up."

I moved to the end of the bench so I didn't have to listen to him. He was still criticizing Hank, even though we were winning.

Rob scored another goal, and the game was over. Everyone was smacking Oscar on the back, telling him how much he'd helped with the win. I was happy for him, but not so happy for me. I tried not to let it show.

"You really helped the team today," I told Oscar on the way home.

"Yeah, it was fun being out there more than ten minutes," he said.

"I'm getting sick of sitting on that bench, I can tell you, especially with Ray there with me," I said.

"I never thought I'd get any playing time," he said. "My school in Colorado was a lot bigger than here. I'd never have had the chance to play."

"Hey, you wanna come in and meet Ivan?" he asked when we got to his house.

"Ivan who?"

I'd met his mom and three little sisters at one of the first soccer games, but he'd never mentioned an Ivan in the family.

"He's our family pet. Ivan's pretty smart, but I don't think he's as smart as Mac."

"Sure, but I can only stay a few minutes. I have to get home to let Mac out."

Oscar's sisters sat at the kitchen table. Three blonde heads bent over the table covered with paper, paints, and glue.

"Hey, Angela, will you go get Ivan?" Oscar asked his youngest sister.

"I'm busy, Oscar," she said. "Kate can get him." Angela was missing two front teeth, and she talked with a lisp.

"Be careful taking him out of the cage, Kate. Put his leash on," Oscar said.

Cage? Leash?

I didn't have to wonder long. Kate came back with a large iguana pulling her along. I wasn't real fond of reptiles. This one's tongue darted in and out, as if he'd like to take a bite of my leg. I stepped back quickly, nearly tripping over the chair. Ivan also had a strange odor, like he bathed in a swamp.

"Don't worry." Oscar took the leash. "He's just curious. He won't bite you. We keep him on a leash because he'd get loose and wander around. A fox or dog could attack him."

I knew Mac would never go near Ivan. He'd take one look at that darting tongue and take off. Maybe some fox would be brave enough, but I doubted it.

"See, he likes you," Angela said.

The iguana poked at my shoes. A tingle started up my leg.

"Ah, I'd better get going. I've got to let Mac out," I said.

I breathed a lot easier when the door closed behind me, leaving the miniature monster on the other side.

No, thanks. Give me a dog any day, even one who climbs fences.

*   *   *   *

The soccer field wasn't the only place I didn't play a starring role in my life.

Even with all the reading help, school hadn't gotten any easier. It took me so long to do my homework that I'd fall asleep at my desk. I was still struggling with reading the long words. I'd gotten better at the shorter ones, but not too many books use all short words, especially not social studies.

That class was my worst nightmare. Mr. Sparks assigned us an end-of-term project, which would count for one third of our grade. He decided we should do the projects in groups and put Ray, Chrissie, Oscar, and me together. Sparks might've known a lot about social studies, but he was clueless about social relations.

Chrissie and I had been friends since fourth grade, when we were in Learning Center together. She could read just fine but needed help in math. Back then, she looked a little like Oscar. She had fewer freckles, but she had bright red pigtails that stuck out on the side of her head.

She'd changed a lot since fourth grade. Her hair was a deeper red, not bright anymore, and it was long and shiny. Chrissie laughed a lot, and when she laughed, you'd want to stop and listen. It sounded sort of musical, not like the screeching giggling of the other girls.

I sat behind her in social studies, and Ray sat on the other side of the room. He was always hanging over her desk before class, but she chose me as a partner when we had to read aloud. She'd whisper the harder words to me so I wouldn't stumble over them when my turn came.

When I saw her with Ray that day after practice, I felt really bad. How could she have anything to do with Ray?

After he set up the groups, Sparks chose one person from each group to read. He picked me. As soon as he called my name, Chrissie raised her hand.

"Could I read for our group, Mr. Sparks?" she asked. "I'm really interested in this section about Native Americans."

"Yeah, and dummy here can't read," Ray said loud enough for everyone but Sparks to hear.

Enough! I jumped out of my seat and headed toward him. "I'm no dumber than you are, 'honey,'" I said.

"Who are you calling 'honey?'" he asked. He stood up at his desk and straight-armed me. I fell backward between the desks. I looked up, and Chrissie and Oscar stared down at me with their mouths wide open.

I scrambled to my feet and headed for the door. "You're a lousy goalie too!" I yelled as I bolted from the room.

I ran down the corridor, out of the building, straight across the soccer field, and into the woods.

I hydroplaned along the path, bounding over the bulging stumps criss-crossing it. I was conscious only of the sound of the wind whistling in my ears and the rasp of my breathing. I kept running. No voice called after me. No feet pounded down the path to snatch me back to the torture that was Ray Quinn and Granite Cove Middle School.

"Run away. Run away. Run away," chanted in my ears, breaking the rhythm of the humming wind, keeping time to the motion of my legs, the touch of my feet on the dirt path. When I reached the cliff over the ocean, I stopped. Rolling waves broke on the rocks below. Salt spray shot into the air.

I sat down on a rock, watching the water retreat back again to gather strength to pound against the shore once more.

Stupid; I'm just stupid, I thought. But I'm not. Ray is the one who's stupid. How can Chrissie be his girlfriend? How can she call that creep "honey?"

I couldn't figure that one out, but I had finally shown Ray that I was through letting him bad-mouth and bully me. I'd stood up to him. Finally, after all those years of turning away, I'd told him off. I didn't know what Ray would do to get back at me, but I was ready, whatever it was.

I walked back down the path, cut over to the road to avoid the school, and headed for home. I hoped school had left a message saying I was suspended. I would have liked a couple of days off to let the dust settle.

I hadn't thought about my parents' reaction. Before I got to my house, my father drove down the road. He stopped and motioned for me to get in the truck. Just by his face and white-knuckled grip on the steering wheel, I knew that he knew.

He didn't say anything until we got to the house. The silence sucked the air out of the car. When he pulled into the driveway, he shut off the engine and turned to me.

"I've been driving around looking for you for the last hour, Jamie."

"Why? You knew I'd come home eventually."

"I certainly hoped so, but I wasn't about to wait around to find out," he said.

He acted mad and disappointed. I could deal better with mad.

"Your principal, Mr. Simmons, called the house and said you had left school in the middle of the day without permission. He said if you didn't show up within an hour, he'd have to call the police."

"Why would he call the police?"

"It's school policy. I want you to go into the house, call Mr. Simmons, and tell him you're at home. I'll speak to him when you finish."

Mr. Simmons just sounded mad.

"You have a two-day in-school suspension, Jamie. I expect to see you in my office before school tomorrow."

Oscar called when he got home from practice.

"Good for you, Jamie," he said. "You finally showed Quinn you wouldn't take his garbage. Everyone in the class was on your side—even Sparks, I think. Boy, was he flustered for the rest of the period."

"I looked like a jerk, though, running out of class. They gave me an in-school suspension. I couldn't even get a few days away from that place," I said.

"Yeah, but if you'd been suspended, you probably couldn't play soccer. Maybe with an 'in-school,' you'll still be able to practice."

"I doubt it."

"Chrissie stuck up for you," Oscar told me. "She told Mr. Sparks what Ray said. He sent him to the office. He probably has an 'in-school' too. I'm pretty sure he isn't Chrissie's 'honey' anymore."

Great! Not only was I going to have to go back to school in the morning, but I might be spending the next two days sitting across a table in the guidance office with Ray. It would be worth it, though, if Chrissie finally saw Ray for the creep that he was.

Chapter Six

I expected a long lecture when I got to school, but Mr. Simmons just told me to go to Mrs. Hogan's room for both days of the suspension.

I should have been happy. I wouldn't have to see Ray or anyone else, but how could I survive a whole day of reading classes?

I didn't have to. I had my regular class with Mrs. H. While she was teaching her other classes, I listened to short stories on a tape recorder and timed how fast I could read them. Then I answered questions at the end of each story. I wished I could do that every day during reading class instead of that boring syllable stuff.

"Good work, Jamie," she said at the end of the day. "You're reading much better. I'm glad you didn't quit on me at the beginning of the year."

I didn't tell her I would have if my father hadn't nixed the idea. I wasn't so sure I was reading all that much better. I had been tapping out the sounds and breaking the words into syllables, but lots of times, I broke them in the wrong places.

"Maybe, but I still can't read like the other kids."

"In time, you will," she said. "But you have to come to my class every day. My attendance book says you've missed four classes over the past three weeks. I checked at the office, and their records say you were in school those days. You need to bring an excuse when you miss a class." She stopped for a minute and looked out the window.

"I'm sorry about what happened in your social studies class yesterday," she continued. "You need to get over your fear of reading in class and learn how to handle people like Ray." She turned and looked at me with those piercing black eyes. "There are a lot of Rays in this world, you know."

I sure hoped not. One Ray was enough.

At the end of the day, I felt better than I had when I'd dragged myself to school that morning.

It didn't take long for my bubble to burst.

Mr. Bracken stopped me outside of homeroom on my way out of the building.

"I've got to drop these papers off at the office, Jamie. Wait for me in my classroom."

"Ah, I have soccer practice," I said.

"Not today," he said. "No after-school sports when you're suspended, in-school or out-of-school."

I sweated out waiting for him to come back. It didn't take long. He came in and shut the door.

"I was surprised at the incident between you and Ray, Jamie. I know Ray's mouth gets him into trouble, but you shouldn't let it get you into trouble too. Learn to ignore him."

Easy for you to say, I thought.

"I just got my midterm reports from the office this morning. You're getting warnings in both English and social studies."

Bracken rocked back-and-forth in his desk chair, tapping his teeth with a pencil. He always tapped his teeth with that pencil. It was annoying. I wondered why his teeth weren't black from all that lead, but his pearly whites gleamed right at me.

I could feel the headache banging away at the back of my head. Midterm reports were a warning, or just another way of saying, "Hey, kid, you're going to flunk."

"I know you have difficulty reading," his voice cut in. "But your teachers say you don't turn in homework and you don't pay attention in class."

That was not true. Just because I stared out the window didn't mean I wasn't paying attention. I listened real hard in class, and I almost always did my homework.

Lockers slammed in the hall. Bracken stood up. I turned to leave, hoping he was through.

"That's not all, Jamie. Mrs. Hogan tells me you've missed some tutoring sessions and haven't brought in an excuse." He crossed his arms and leaned back in his chair. The urge to run was strong.

"Ah, I've been getting headaches again. I went to the nurse's office, and I forgot to …"

"Look, Jamie," he interrupted. "You have to let teachers know when you're not in class. The nurse will give you a note. You'll have one after-school detention for each day you missed with Mrs. Hogan. I'll call your parents to let them know about the warnings and that you've missed a few classes."

I couldn't believe this. I couldn't go to practice for two days just because I'd finally told Ray off, and three detentions would mean

I'd be late for practice three more days. Coach would *not* be happy. This would pretty much end my hope for any playing time in goal this season.

Oscar waited outside, shivering in the damp cold of the late fall afternoon.

"Practice was canceled," he said. "Coach had to go to the dentist or something. I saw you going into Bracken's classroom after school, and I figured I'd wait for you."

"I got a couple of warnings," I told him. "Bracken wants to talk to my parents. He said if I get an F on my report card, I can't play on any after-school sports team until I pull my grade up. That's not all. He gave me four detentions for missing some of my reading classes. I'll miss five practices in a row."

"That's not good," Oscar said. "We only have four weeks of soccer left."

"No kidding."

"I got a midterm in science," Oscar said. "Smith told me after class, but he didn't tell me about after-school sports."

"I had you figured for an all-A kind of guy," I said. I felt better knowing Oscar had gotten a warning too. "I thought you were a real brainiac."

"Nah. My dad had the brains in our family. I just don't get some of those experiments in science."

"Science and math are the only classes where I don't feel stupid," I said. "I like numbers—the way they line up when you add them. Six apples is six apples—add two, you get eight, multiply the six apples five times, you get thirty. That makes sense to me."

"I need to see things to understand them. When we do experiments in science, I can see what's happening. Or like knowing that clouds hold water, and if there are enough clouds and they get full enough, then we'll have rain. Easy."

I thought about how much I'd learned about nature and the weather from my dad. Maybe he couldn't read real well, but he sure was smart about practical stuff.

"Maybe we should do homework together sometimes," Oscar said. "I can help with the English and social studies, and you can help me with science."

"Maybe," I said. I didn't really want him to hear me stumbling over the words when I read.

I left Oscar at his house and walked as slowly as I could the rest of the way home. By then, Bracken had probably called my parents. My mother would have that sad, worried look on her face, and my dad would probably be mad.

They'd never had a phone call about me in elementary school. This week they had two.

"Sit down, Jamie," Dad said.

They were at the kitchen table, having a cup of coffee.

"Mr. Bracken called to let us know you're getting two warnings and that you hadn't been showing up for reading help."

Thank you, Mr. B.

Dad sounded calm—too calm. When he was angry, he got red in the face and shouted, and Mac would run under the table.

"You're a good kid and a hard worker, Jamie," he said. "You are a real help to me on the boat. This fighting and not doing your work is hard for your mother and me to understand. We're disappointed in you."

"I didn't fight, Dad. Ray pushed me."

"That's not the point, Jamie. You have two days of in-school suspension because you had a confrontation with another kid and ran out of school in the middle of the day; now we find out that you've been skipping classes. This has to stop."

"Mr. Bracken said you should definitely see the reading tutor every day and start going to Homework Club after school," Mom added.

"But I'll miss soccer practice."

"Right now, your school work is more important than soccer," she said.

"I could study with Oscar. He does good in all his classes except science," I said. "If I help him with science, he'll help me with English and social studies. We can work together every day after practice. Can we try that until soccer is over? If my report card isn't good, I'll start going to Homework Club then."

"That won't work, Jamie," Dad said. "Starting tomorrow, we expect you to go to tutoring and Homework Club every day."

I felt that lump of ice melting in my stomach again.

CHAPTER SEVEN

With an hour of Homework Club added on to a full day of classes, the day was very long and very boring. Coach let me come to the last half of soccer practice, and I had my ten minutes of play every game, but it wasn't enough. I was getting frustrated.

I'd gotten a seventy-five on a book report in English and a sixty-seven on a social studies quiz. We had a final paper due in social studies that counted as two grades. It was my only chance to bring up my average.

Since the Ray, Chrissie, Oscar, and Jamie combination hadn't worked out, Oscar and I were doing the project together. We were having a hard time coming up with a topic. It had to have something to do with Native Americans.

Oscar and I were up in my bedroom tossing ideas around, when Mac jumped on the bed and knocked a box of arrowheads off the shelf.

"Hey, where'd you get these?" Oscar asked, picking them up one-by-one and examining them.

"Mac was chasing a rabbit out in the woods, and it escaped into a hole. He started to dig and uncovered an arrowhead. I kept going and found the rest."

"Why didn't you think of this before?" Oscar asked. "Indians and arrowheads go together like ham and cheese, peanut butter and jelly ..."

"Okay. Okay," I said. "I get it. I just forgot about them."

When Oscar was excited, his face got as red as his hair, and he kind of rolled back-and-forth on his toes like he was going to jump up in the air.

I held one of the hard stone arrowheads up to the light and rubbed my hand along the ridge in the middle. Most of the others weren't in very good shape—tips broken or the ridge chipped away—but this one was in good condition.

"Did you ever show the arrowheads to anybody? I mean, people are interested in these things." Oscar sat down on the bed and rubbed his finger along the edge of the arrowhead. "My dad would have liked to see them. He could probably have told us the name of the tribe and when they lived here."

Oscar hadn't mentioned his father in a long time. I think if my dad died, I'd have to talk about him to someone. Oscar just got quiet once in a while. I figured he was thinking about his dad.

"Do you remember where you found these?" he asked.

"They were right behind the big rock where the trail into South Woods starts. I bet I could find it again."

"We don't really need to find more arrowheads," Oscar said. "We'll just show the ones you have. I bet the historical museum has lots of stuff about the Indians who lived around here."

After school on Monday, we went to the museum. Nobody came when we rang the bell.

"This says the museum is only open on Sundays, except in the summer." Oscar pointed to a sign next to the door.

"We're supposed to give the report on Friday. We're fried," I said.

We turned away and started back down the granite steps.

"We're closed," a voice hollered as we shut the front gate.

"We know. We just read the sign," Oscar said to the elderly man standing in the doorway. He had a mop in one hand and a pail in the other.

"We're giving a report on the Indians who lived around here, and we thought we could get some information at the museum."

"Come back Sunday," the man said. "Indians come from India. The folks you're talking about are called Native Americans." He turned away.

"We have these arrowheads that my friend found." Oscar held out the box.

The man put down the mop and pail and came out on the steps.

"Where'd you find these?" He frowned at us as if we might have stolen them.

"My dog and I dug them up near the big rock at the entrance to the trail into South Woods," I said.

"When?" He pushed his face right up to mine. I could see the stubble of his gray beard and smell something like sardines on his breath.

"Last spring," I answered, stepping back as the aroma of his lunch hit me.

"Why didn't you bring them here?" he demanded, looking at each of us with that unfriendly frown.

"I don't know. I guess I just didn't think to."

He grabbed the box from Oscar and sat down on the steps to examine each arrowhead.

"Well, boys, you certainly found some genuine arrowheads. If I'm not mistaken, they look like the ones inside that were dug up from around Gull Beach."

"Name's Pete," he said, opening the door to the museum. "Usually give the tours, but the floors needed washing today."

He led us to a glass case full of arrowheads and tools.

"These were dug up from all around Cape Ann," he said.

There were about twenty stone tools in the case: flat, blunt stones used for hoes, a long, slim stone that looked like a knife, and a lot more arrowheads.

"Over in that case there are stone weights and bone hooks used for fishing." Pete pointed to a smaller case across the room.

The weights looked a lot like the ones we use today.

"Who gave you all these?" I asked.

"Lots of folks around here have been interested in the natives and in archaeology. You know what that is, don't you boys?"

"I think so," Oscar answered. "It's digging for things the people who were here before us left behind, like pots and stuff."

"More or less," Pete said. "Come on upstairs. We've got some books that might interest you."

He took some books down from a shelf, but before we opened any of them, we peppered him with questions.

"What were the Native Americans around here called?" Oscar asked Pete.

"The Pawtuckets," he answered.

"When did they first come here?" Oscar asked.

"A long time ago," Pete said. "From some of these tools, they've figured out they'd been here about eleven thousand years."

"And the Europeans came in the 1600s?" I said.

"The English came in the 1600s, but the Spanish came in the early 1500s. By the time the English settled and cleared the land, most of the natives had died from smallpox."

"How did they get smallpox?" I asked.

"The natives had no immunity to the diseases the Europeans brought with them. They had been here for thousands of years, and in less than a hundred, white men managed to nearly wipe them out."

"Do any of their descendants still live around here?" Oscar asked.

"Not so you could tell," he answered. "Some of them moved further north, but most of them intermarried. Their traditions and culture just faded out. Sad, really."

"So what happened when the Europeans came and settled on their land?" Oscar asked.

"Native Americans didn't think of land as something to be owned," Pete said. "They lived near the ocean to fish and grow vegetables in the summer, and then they moved inland to hunt for meat in the winter."

"One of the local chiefs, Masconomet, sold ten thousand acres of land to the settlers for seven pounds," Pete continued. "He didn't have any idea when he sold them the land that the settlers would fence most of it in and not let the natives hunt or fish on it anymore."

"Seven pounds doesn't sound like much money to me," I said.

"It wasn't," Pete said. "That would be about $1,000 now. Some of you kids probably spend that on a fancy bicycle today."

"I don't understand how the settlers could keep them from fishing and hunting on land that had been their home," Oscar said. "Sounds pretty unfair. It's like they stole the land."

"It wasn't fair, but it took history a while to figure that out," Pete agreed.

We listened to Pete for two hours, scribbling notes as he talked. It began to get dark, so we headed home.

*   *   *   *

The report was due on Friday. We worked on it every day after Homework Club and soccer. Oscar spelled better than I did, so we used the computer at his house. He typed while I struggled to read the notes we'd taken at the museum. We finished it late Thursday afternoon.

The phone rang at about nine o'clock, just as I was beginning to fall asleep. It was Oscar.

"You're not going to believe this," he said. "Kate forgot to lock Ivan's cage this afternoon after she took him for a walk. He got out and went into my bedroom while we were eating dinner."

I knew I didn't want to hear what was coming next.

"I left the report on the floor, and Ivan shredded almost all of it."

"But you saved it, didn't you?" I asked.

"Most of it," he said.

"Most of it?" I shouted.

"Take it easy," he said. "I forgot to save the last two pages, but I pretty much remember what we wrote. I'll have it ready for tomorrow."

I didn't sleep too well that night, but Oscar came to school in the morning with the report in his hands.

"Had you worried, didn't I?" he asked with a big grin.

That wasn't the end of worrying about the report.

Before we went to lunch, we left the report and arrowheads in homeroom. When we went back to get them afterward, they were gone. We looked inside all the desks, on the floor, and on Mr. Bracken's desk.

"Don't panic. It's here someplace. Maybe Mr. Bracken took it." I could taste the hot dog I'd eaten for lunch marching back up my throat.

"We don't have time to look for him. We're late for class already," Oscar said. "We'll just tell Mr. Sparks what happened. He'll understand."

We rushed down the empty hall to class. I had my doubts that Sparks would believe us. He wasn't the most understanding teacher I'd ever had.

"Late slip?" Sparks held out his hand.

"Uh, no, uh … we were looking for our report," I said.

"You're supposed to be giving it right now."

We tried to explain what happened, but he wasn't buying the story.

"Unless you're ready on Monday, you'll have to take an F for the project," he said.

My head began to pound.

Mr. Bracken wasn't in his homeroom after school.

"We'll wait until he comes back," Oscar said.

Bracken hadn't seen the reports or the arrowheads.

"Are you sure you left them in this room?" he asked.

He looked at us as if we were making all this up because we hadn't done the report.

"We're sure." We both answered together.

"Well, they couldn't have just disappeared," he said. "I have to go to a meeting. Keep looking. They must be here somewhere. Hope you find them."

"Who would take our report and the arrowheads?" Oscar asked.

We looked at each other.

"Did you see Ray at lunch?" he asked.

"Yeah. I saw him sitting with Rob Cody. Then I saw them outside dribbling a soccer ball," I said.

"That lets him out."

"Did you save the report last night after Ivan messed it up?" I asked.

He didn't answer right away.

"Oscar?" I glared at him. "It's in your computer, right?"

His face began to get red and he started rocking back and forth on his toes.

We hopped on our bikes, raced to his house, ran up to his bedroom, and turned on the computer. It took forever to boot up. I paced around the room while Oscar sat at the computer biting his nails.

"It's here!" Oscar yelled and pointed to the screen. I knew it was."

"Yeah, sure you did," I said.

I was relieved, but I felt bad about losing the arrowheads.

"We probably won't get as good a mark without the arrowheads," I said.

"No, but we won't get and F," he said.

"Did you give your report yesterday?" Dad asked on the way to the boat the next morning.

I hadn't told him we'd lost the report and the arrowheads.

"Ah, no. We're doing it on Monday."

"I liked to go to that museum when I was a kid," he said. "There was a guy there who used to take groups of kids along the coast to dig for arrowheads and tools. "I went with him once, but we didn't find anything."

"I can remember him telling us that when the natives fished these waters, there used to be so many fish that the settlers could walk through the shallow water with cod, herring, and mackerel swimming around their legs."

We could put that in our report, I thought.

We pulled up next to the first buoy and emptied the trap, but there were only a couple of keepers in it. The season was winding down.

CHAPTER EIGHT

The report and the arrowheads were still missing on Monday. Sparks gave us a B on the second report.

"Your report was interesting," Chrissie told me after class. "I never knew anything about the Native Americans who lived around here."

"Not as interesting as it would have been if I'd had the arrowheads," I said, "but thanks."

Chrissie had dropped Ray. He and I were avoiding each other. He'd stopped the Oscar/Big Bird routine, but I still didn't trust him.

Grades had closed, and I sweated out waiting for the report card to come in the mail.

"I have something here you might like to see," my mother said when I walked in from school the next Monday. She was smiling. I reached for the envelope. The A in math and D+ in social studies jumped out at me. I hadn't flunked anything.

"I'm proud of you, Jamie. You worked hard. I know it hasn't been easy," she said.

It sure hadn't. Listening to soccer practice right outside the Homework-Club window made it hard to concentrate.

"The soccer playoffs are next week. Can I go to practice instead of staying after school to do my homework?" I asked.

"We can talk that over with Dad tonight."

"When's he comin' home?"

"He's at a meeting with the Lobsterman's Association, but he'll be home for dinner."

That was at least two hours away, so Mac and I went for a run in the woods.

My mother was reading my report card to my father when I came into the kitchen. I'd begun to notice that she read lots of things to him, like menus and stuff.

"Looks like your hard work is paying off, Jamie," he said.

"But, Dad, the soccer playoffs are next week, and I won't be able to practice or go to the games if I have to stay after school to do my homework."

After all that work, I'd still miss soccer. It just wasn't fair.

"You can go to soccer practice next week, but you'll have to go back to Homework Club after the playoffs are finished." he said.

＊　　＊　　＊　　＊

On Saturday morning, Mom suggested I finish raking the leaves.

"Snow will be coming soon," she said. "Better get them done now."

"But I need to help Dad on the boat."

"Not today," she said.

When I was a little kid, I loved when my dad raked the leaves and I jumped in the piles. It wasn't as much fun when it was my job.

The leaves were damp and heavy and smelled like dirty socks mixed with rotten apples. Mac ran through the piles and scattered the wet, shriveled mess all over the lawn, until I finally put him in the house.

Sam and Jake came by on their bikes while I was putting the last bag in the barn.

"Hey, wanna go downtown to see what's happening?" Sam asked, balancing on his back wheel and turning in a circle.

"Nothing's happening, Sam," I said. "Nothing ever happens after the tourists go home. There's nobody to laugh at."

"Nah, but the ice-cream store is still open," Jake said.

"I guess that's enough reason to go. We can stop and pick up Oscar on the way," I said.

Oscar waited for us at the end of his driveway.

"Hey, that was a good move when you practically ran under the legs of the Rocket's winger yesterday." Jake said. "The kid did a face-plant in the middle of the field. Too bad they called a foul on you."

"Yeah, but he didn't get a chance to score," Oscar grinned.

Oscar's sisters were at the ice-cream store when we got there.

"I don't have enough money," Angela said.

"She needs a quarter," Kate told us. "I think she dropped one someplace."

Oscar fished in his pocket and came up with fifteen cents. Sam had a dime.

"They don't look anything like you," Sam said as the three curly-headed blondes walked away. "Too bad you didn't get their hair."

"Hey, I like my hair. Makes me stand out in a crowd," Oscar said.

We sat on one of the benches on the common watching the tiny world of Granite Cove village. The tourists hadn't all gone home. There were still a lot of them eating ice cream and walking in front of cars. It was kind of fun to watch. You had to wonder how people could be so clueless; like, didn't they see the cars?

I got up to throw the rest of my cone in the trash barrel. Three bikes were speeding down Mt. Pleasant hill. They were headed right in the direction of Oscar's sisters, who were crossing the street. I could see a Dolphins hat in the lead. Ray. It was like watching a movie in slow motion.

"Watch out!" I yelled.

Kate turned and saw the bikes heading toward them. The girls started to run. Angela tripped and fell.

The bikes screeched to a halt. Ray Quinn dropped his bike and ran to where Angela had fallen.

Oscar knelt down beside his sister. "Are you okay? Did you get hit?"

"We didn't hit her. We saw her," Ray said.

"Where's my ice cream?" Angela wanted to know.

"See, she's okay," Ray said.

Oscar jumped up and went toward Ray, with Sam, Jake, and I right behind him.

"Okay, boys, I'll handle this." Sergeant Rowe pulled up beside us in one of Granite Cove's gray and-blue police trucks.

"What happened?"

We all started to talk at once.

"One at a time, please. Let's start with you." He pointed to Oscar.

"These jerks were speeding down the hill, not looking where they were going. My sisters were crossing the street, and one of them almost hit Angela."

Angela sat on the curb, picking gravel off her ruined ice cream cone.

"That's not true," Ray said. "We didn't hit her. We stopped as soon as we saw them."

Rowe bent down next to Angela. "Are you hurt, little lady?" he asked.

"No, but I fell and dropped my ice cream." Tears started running down her cheeks.

"Did you hurt yourself when you fell?" he asked.

"I can't eat my ice cream," she wailed.

"I'll tell you what." Rowe bent down to talk to Angela. "As soon as I get this sorted out, we'll get you another ice cream."

He stood up and turned to us. "Who was riding the bikes?" he asked.

"We were," the "three stooges" answered at the same time.

"Okay, then. I want the rest of you to get this little girl another ice cream while I talk to these gentlemen."

"I'm staying with my sisters," Oscar said.

"Ah, we don't have any money," I said.

Sergeant Rowe reached into his pocket and handed us a couple of bills.

When we got back, Ray and his buddies were walking up Main Street. Their bikes were in the cab of the police truck.

I gave Angela the ice cream cone, and handed the change back to Rowe. Her tears were long gone. Kate and Mary Beth looked with envy at their little sister happily eating her second ice-cream cone.

"So what happened?" Jake asked Oscar.

"He took their bikes and told them they could have them back when they came to the police station with their parents," Oscar said with a big grin.

"Serves them right," Sam said. "He's been asking for trouble. Now he's got it."

"Ray's a jerk, but I wouldn't want to be him right now," I said to Oscar on the way home. "His stepfather's mean. He's big and bald with a scruffy beard and built like one of those guys who wrestle on television."

"At one of the soccer games last summer, he screamed at Ray for letting in a goal, and I saw him cuff him on the side of the head as they left the field."

"I see what you mean," Oscar said.

Maybe his stepfather is part of the reason Ray is a bully, I thought.

*   *   *   *

The league championship would be decided in the best two out of three games. We beat the Falcons in the first game and lost the second.

Ray came to school, but he didn't talk to anybody. He didn't show up for soccer, either.

The final game was Saturday.

Coach called me Friday night to tell me that Hank was sick.

"It looks like you'll be in goal tomorrow, Jamie. You are going to be there, aren't you?"

"Yeah, sure."

"Good. We're counting on you," he said.

"I'm in goal!" I shouted, jumping around the room. Mac hopped up on the bed to get out of the way.

"What's all the noise?" Mom came into my room.

"I'm playing in tomorrow's game," I said. "Hank is sick. I mean, I'm sorry he's sick and all, but it's the last game, and I haven't been in goal all year."

"Good for you," she said.

I hadn't played a whole game since the summer, and this was for the league championship. I went to bed early, but I couldn't sleep. I tossed and turned so much that Mac jumped off the bed and slept on the floor.

The game wasn't until one o'clock. I woke up early, so I went with Dad to haul a few pots around the harbor. We got back before noon. I forced down a sandwich and a glass of milk and left for the field. I was the first one there, but Oscar and Jake showed up just as I finished lacing my cleats.

"Hank's sick, 'honey' is in trouble, and I bet you're in goal today," Oscar said.

"Who's 'honey?'" Jake asked.

Oscar told him the "Ray-honey" story.

"I wonder what happened to those guys when their parents found out," Jake said.

"Ray hasn't been at soccer all week," Oscar said.

"I bet they won't be riding those bikes again real soon," Jake added.

"Want some practice?" Jake asked as the rest of the team began coming onto the field to warm up.

Jake showed me no mercy, but I stopped most of his shots. Rob Cody lined up about twenty yards out and took a straight shot right down the center. I came out of the goal to stop it. The ball curved to my left. I dove for it and smothered it.

"Great save, Parker," Rob said.

The Falcons arrived. Coach called us over for some pre-game instructions.

"I want you to stay around the goal, Jamie. Don't wander or stray from that area," he told me.

"Nervous?" Jake asked.

"Not any more than usual," I said. "Besides, a little nervous is good."

The bleachers started to fill. Mom waved to me. I didn't see my dad, but I knew he was coming.

The referee blew his whistle. We won the toss. Jon Shaw, the center forward, dribbled around the defenders and passed the ball to Joey Petrano, the right wing. Joey ran forward and kicked the ball downfield to Rob. He pulled his foot back and aimed it toward the right side of the goal. The goalie moved over. Rob angled his shot to the left, kicking the ball into the goal. Score. First goal for us!

Above the roar of the crowd, I concentrated on the Falcons' striker rushing toward me with the ball. He passed it to their right wing. Oscar was on him, but he moved to the left, made a quick kick into the corner, and they scored.

The game heated up. Players on both teams hustled after the ball, but Rob kept control of it. He passed it to Joey. Joey dribbled it down the left side of the field and passed it back to Rob in front of the goal. Rob kicked it lightly, and it dribbled into the net. 2–1, our lead.

On the next play, the Falcons' striker moved downfield, passing the ball to his right wing. I yelled to the defense to move in front of the right side of the goal. I moved to the left. Save!

The Falcons' midfielder kicked the ball downfield. His striker was ahead of it. Our defense rushed forward, but the striker threaded between the defenders, drew his foot back, and took a straight shot right into the goal. 2–2. It was an easy shot, and I missed it.

The whistle blew for halftime—tie score.

"You're doing fine, Jamie," Coach said. "Remember, a goalie is only as good as his defense. I want the rest of you to stay focused, move the ball, and try to keep it in their end as much as possible."

"I want you to cover their right wing, Oscar. The rest of you stay in your zones."

Coach put Jake in for the first ten minutes of the second half. Rob came back in, dribbled the ball past midfield; passed it to Oscar, and ran ahead. The Falcons' winger tackled Oscar from behind. He didn't get up.

The crowd got quiet. Coach went out on the field. After what seemed like a long time, Oscar stood up. He limped off the field. The referee called a foul on the Falcons' right wing.

We had a penalty shot. Rob lined the ball up on the right side of the box, drew his foot back, and kicked. The ball hit the post and came back out.

None of the players on either team managed to put the ball in the net. The whistle blew on a tie score. The game went into sudden-death overtime. The Falcons quickly pressured us, but I made a save on a long shot.

On the next play, Rob threaded through the defensive line, pulled his foot back, and kicked from about ten yards out. Goal!

Score 3–2. The Hornets swarmed onto the field and carried Rob off on their shoulders.

"We did it." Jake pummeled me on the back.

"Yes, we did," I said.

"Great game, Jamie," Chrissie Young called across the field.

Chapter Nine

The last week of soccer had given me a chance to take a break from worrying about school, but with soccer over, I felt like I was right back where I started.

The books on tape helped in English. But reading class was up-and-down. I'd reach a certain point and feel like I was doing good, and then I'd get to a harder part and struggle again. It was frustrating, and I was getting discouraged.

At least when I played soccer, I had something to look forward to, even if I had a bad day in school.

I think Mrs. H., like my mother, could read my mind.

"Don't get discouraged, Jamie. You've made good progress. Your last testing was almost a year ago. I'll test you again in a few weeks, and I think you'll be surprised at how much you've gained in the past months."

Maybe, but I wasn't convinced.

Ray was back to his old self. I wished Mr. Bracken would move him from the front row in homeroom. Whenever he knew he wouldn't be caught, Ray stuck his legs out to trip anyone going past.

He tripped Oscar one morning, and he fell right into Ray's lap. Oscar sat up, put his arms around Ray, and hugged him. The whole room broke up. Old Ray was pretty red in the face.

Mr. Bracken never seemed to be in the room when any of this happened.

With soccer over, I had time to work with my father on Saturdays.

"Lobsterin's comin' to a close for this year," he said a couple of weeks before Christmas. "The cold is drivin' the lobsters into hibernation early. The past couple of years, I've been able to work the traps until the middle of January."

"This was a pretty good year, though. I set out eight hundred pots, and we managed to get a good haul from most of them."

"Does that mean you won't have to sell your boat?"

"I'm not plannin' to," he said.

"Next year, I'd like to buy my own boat and get a ten-pot license," I said. "I've been saving up, and Ollie has a skiff he'll sell to me."

"I'll still need you on the boat most of the summer," Dad said. "You can pull your pots when we finish for the day."

The air changed suddenly. A wind came up, and we headed in. At this time of year, the storms usually took a while to build, but it was better to be off the water.

"I remember my first boat," Dad said as we were unloading pots at the dock. "I was younger than you, though not by much. I was probably ten or so. It was a small double-ended skiff. When I was in high school, my dad helped me buy a bigger boat with an outboard motor. The next boat was bigger, with an inboard. Now I've got this fiberglass monster that eats up gas that costs more every day."

I liked to hear my father talk about when he was a kid, and I liked to hear the older fishermen tell their tales. They had some stories to tell!

In the winter, I would go down to the fishing shacks, where the men sat around the wood stove repairing traps or just talking. There was a smell of wet wool mixed with fish and pipe tobacco. Kinda like fishermens' perfume.

On the way home, we stopped at the pond across from Oscar's house to see if the ice was frozen. We'd had three or four cold days in a row, but there was still only a skim of ice on the pond. Mac headed toward the water.

I ran after him and caught his collar before he got there. Mac loved running and sliding across the ice.

"You've gotta keep an eye on that guy," Dad said. "He might just decide he'd like to go skating, and the ice isn't quite ready yet."

We didn't usually have skating ice until Christmas week or after, but we had a few more days of real cold weather, and the ice looked solid by the end of the next week.

"I'm going skating on the pond tomorrow," I told Oscar after school the next Friday. "Wanna come?"

"I can't skate," he said. "We always went skiing, so I never learned how to skate."

"If you can ski, you can skate," I told him.

The next afternoon, I brought him a pair of my old skates, and we went down to the pond. Mac came, too.

Oscar looked like Mac slipping and sliding across the ice.

I dragged a few logs from around the edge of the pond and made a goal. I took some shots.

"Hey, Oscar, you need to take some lessons." I looked up on the bank and saw Ray lacing up his skates.

Oscar wobbled around the edge of the pond. Mac ran beside him like a coach.

"Want me to shoot a few at you?" Ray asked.

What was this? Was he really looking to play a little hockey or for a chance to bean me with a puck? I just didn't get it. Ray was talking to me in a normal voice, like a normal person, which I knew he wasn't.

"Come on," he said. "Oscar's not going to be able to handle skating and a hockey stick at the same time." Ray skated into the goal.

Ray Quinn hadn't said a civil word to me since second grade. He had to be up to something. I wasn't sure I wanted to find out what it was.

I lined up the puck and shot it at him. He missed. I shot a few more. He got a few and he missed a few.

"Your turn," he said.

He shot some at me. I stopped a couple and let a couple in. We were about even at that point.

The next shot came at me in the air. I reached up to catch the puck. I caught something, but it wasn't a puck. I looked into my glove and saw an arrowhead. An arrowhead? An ancient arrowhead lay in my glove. I looked up at him. He had a smirk on his face.

I dropped the stick and raced across the ice. He turned and skated away. I dove for his legs. He fell on the ice. I tripped and fell on top of him. Ray tried to crawl toward the edge of the pond. Mac ran after us, barking.

I heard a crack and felt the ice give. Water seeped up my pant legs. Ray scrambled away and made it to the edge.

"Jamie!" Oscar yelled. "Mac's fallen through!"

I looked back. The ice behind me had disappeared. Mac's head stuck out of the water. His paws clawed at the ice, trying to get a grip, but he fell back into the water each time.

"Get help, Oscar!" I shouted. I made it to the bank and pushed my way through the brush at the edge of the pond, trying to find a place that looked solid. Why hadn't I been more careful? Why hadn't I tested the ice? I put one foot out on the ice, trying to find a place where it was firm.

"Go back, Jamie!" Ray shouted. He came across the pond from the opposite direction. "It's solid on this side. I think I can get him."

I could see Ray moving toward Mac. He dropped to the ice and crawled forward on his hands and knees. He reached out to Mac, lifted his head, and slowly pulled him out of the water. I saw Mac's hindquarters land on solid ice. I ran along the edge of the pond, afraid that any minute I would hear the sound of the ice cracking under their weight.

By the time I reached the other side, Ray and Oscar had carried Mac up the bank and laid him by the side of the road. Oscar's mother covered Mac with a blanket.

"You two wrap yourselves up in these," she said and handed Ray and me each a blanket.

"Mom called the police," Oscar said.

Mac's eyes were closed. His whole body shook.

Ray toweled off Mac's head with the edge of his hockey shirt.

Tears streamed down Oscar's face. I was too scared to cry. The sound of a siren wailed in the distance. It felt like forever before the police car pulled up next to us.

"Can you take him to Doc Webber's office?" Oscar's mother asked. "My car wouldn't start this morning."

"Sure can," Lieutenant Santos said.

He wrapped Mac in a silver blanket like the runners wear after a marathon. I held him on my lap. His nose felt as cold as the ice he'd fallen through. I could barely swallow around the lump in my throat.

"This fella's been in the cruiser before," Santos said as we raced toward town. "He used to make the rounds of the coffee shops, begging for leftovers. Sometimes we'd give him a ride home. Haven't seen him around lately, though. Where's he been?"

I could picture Mac walking out of a coffee shop with a doughnut in his mouth.

"We put up a fence. He gets out sometimes, but we don't want him running loose."

I was supposed to be watching him that day. If he died, it would be my fault, I thought as the police car raced toward town.

Doc Webber was operating when we got to the veterinary hospital. The nurse put Mac in a special crib and wrapped him in an electric blanket. She turned on a fan in the corner that blew warm air around the crib.

Finally, Doc came in. "Mac's temperature is very low, Jamie. Right now, I'm concerned about hypothermia, and he could develop some pneumonia."

"But you can give him pills, and he'll get better, right?"

My ears began to ring. I could see Doc's mouth moving, but I didn't really hear the words.

"… Mac's young and healthy. I'll give him antibiotics intravenously, but the next twenty-four hours are critical. He'll have to stay here."

The door opened. My father came into the room. Doc repeated what he'd just told me.

"Can I stay with Mac?" I asked.

"No, Jamie. He'll rest more quietly if you're not here," Doc said.

"We'll check on him through the night." Doc patted me on the shoulder.

"Let's go home, Jamie." My dad's voice broke into the steady whir of the fan.

In the middle of the night, I woke up with a heavy weight pressing down on my chest. I couldn't breathe. At first, I thought it was Mac sitting on me. Then I remembered. I couldn't get back to sleep. Every time I closed my eyes, pictures of Mac in the crib played like a movie on the back of my eyelids.

CHAPTER TEN

It snowed during the night. I woke up to the sound of Dad's truck plowing the driveway. I went downstairs and called Doc Webber.

"He looks a little better this morning," Doc said. "His eyes are open. His temperature is back to normal, and he drank a little water. You can see him whenever you can get here."

The weight in my chest lifted a little, but I had to see for myself. Why did it have to snow today?

I got dressed, grabbed a shovel, and made a path to the driveway. By then, Dad had cleared up to the road. The town plows had come by, but it was slow driving to Doc's.

"We're not going to get there any faster with you sittin' on the edge of your seat like that," Dad said.

Mac was asleep in the crib when we got there. As soon as he heard our voices, he opened his eyes and tried to get up, but he was still very weak. I went over and talked to him. He lay back down, and I sat next to him for about an hour.

"He's better, Jamie," Doc said when he came in to check on Mac. "But he won't rest while you're here, and rest is what he needs."

We brought Mac home on Sunday afternoon. While we ate dinner, he slept on his old bed in the kitchen next to the wood stove. He wasn't moving around much, but Doc said he would recover completely as long as he took it easy for a while—no swimming and no chasing rabbits.

No skating, either, I thought.

Mac shivered every so often. I didn't know whether he was still cold or having a nightmare about trying to climb out of the pond.

I called Oscar and Ray to tell them Mac was home. Ray's stepfather answered.

"I don't know where that kid is. He's useless," his stepfather growled over the phone. "He was supposed to help his mother put up the Christmas tree. He's probably hiding someplace so he doesn't have to do any work."

He hung up the phone without asking who I was or whether Ray should call me back.

I didn't know what to expect from Ray now. He'd saved Mac. I was grateful, but would he still be the old Ray? He had taken the arrowheads, and I wanted them back.

*   *   *   *

Monday morning, Mr. Simmons called me down to the office. Oscar was there. So was Ray. He was sitting in one of the hard plastic chairs Mr. Simmons keeps for students on the hot seat. The room was narrow with one small window over the computer table. Piles of papers frosted the desk. Books stood in piles all over the floor.

"How's Mac?" Ray asked as soon as Oscar and I sat down.

"He's better. Doc says he'll be okay, but he's weak. He hasn't moved far from the wood stove since we brought him home. I called last night to thank you for pulling him out of the pond, but you weren't there."

I still couldn't figure out why Ray, Oscar, and I were all in the principal's office together. Maybe Ray was going to get some kind of commendation for saving Mac.

Mr. Simmons came in and closed the door behind him.

"I had a phone call from someone named Pete at the Historical Museum," he said. "He told me he was looking for some arrowheads that kids from the middle school had brought in; said you were using them for a social studies project. He was hoping you'd donate the arrowheads to the museum, but he couldn't remember your names. I told him I'd look into it."

I looked over at Ray. He was looking down at the floor.

"I asked Mr. Sparks who had done the arrowhead project," Mr. Simmons said. "He told me it was you two. I went to your homeroom, but you weren't there. Ray overheard me talking to Mr. Bracken. He has something he wants to give to you, Jamie."

Ray reached under the chair and pulled out a box. The arrowheads!

"I took these from homeroom that day. They were just sitting on a desk. I kept the arrowheads, but I threw the paper in the wastebasket outside the cafeteria," he said.

I looked over at Oscar. I hadn't told him Ray had shot an arrowhead at me.

Oscar's mouth had dropped open, and if he didn't close it soon, he'd be catching the fly that buzzed around the office.

Why did Ray go and tell the principal? I would have just given them back and stayed out of trouble.

"Sorry," Ray said.

For the first time since I'd know him, Ray sounded like he actually realized he'd done something wrong. I didn't feel as happy as I thought I would to see old Ray humbled.

"It was stupid to take our stuff, but thanks for saving Mac."

"Yeah, that's right," Oscar agreed, shutting his mouth just before the fly buzzed in.

"You guys can go back to class now," Mr. C. said. "Ray and I need to talk."

"Come out and see Mac sometime," I said to Ray. I tucked the box under my arm and closed the door.

Oscar and I high-fived in the hall.

*   *   *   *

Christmas morning, I lay in bed staring at the tic-tac-toe on the ceiling. I thought of how much had happened the past few weeks. I wasn't in a hurry to go downstairs and open presents. Mac was my Christmas present. He was limping a little, but I was just glad he survived. When we were riding in the cruiser on the way to the vet's, I was sure he wouldn't make it.

We opened presents after breakfast. Under the tree, I found a new pair of skates and a goalie stick. My dad handed me a book about hockey. I looked at it and put it down on the coffee table.

"I thought you liked hockey," Dad said, reaching for the book.

"I do, but I don't like reading about it," I said.

"Here, let's try to read it together." He opened the first page and began to read slowly, putting his finger under every word. "You read the next page."

I looked at him. What was this all about?

I read the second page. I had to tap out the sounds of some of the longer words on my fingers.

"I'm learning to do that too," Dad said.

"What?" I asked. "You're learning to do what?"

"I'm learning to tap out the sounds at the reading course I'm taking at the library."

"You're learning to read at the library?" I asked.

"I am. And guess who the teacher is?"

"I haven't a clue," I said.

"Mrs. Hogan." He smiled. "She was the one who suggested I get you that book on hockey."

"No kidding."

"No kidding," he said and got up from the couch. "If I can't make a living catching lobster, knowing how to read will help me get into a job-training program. Besides, I've wanted to read all my life."

My grandparents came just before dinner. There were more presents to open. My grandmother had made dog cookies for Mac.

"Dinner," Mom called from the dining room. I heard Mac's footsteps click across the kitchen floor. He never slept through dinner, especially with the smell of turkey and apple pie in the air.

978-0-595-43915-7
0-595-43915-2